P9-BYO-562

Ripley's
Believe It or Not!
Amazing
Escapes

Look for other

titles:

World's Weirdest Critters
Creepy Stuff
Odd-inary People

by Mary Packard

and the Editors of Ripley Entertainment Inc.

illustrations by Leanne Franson

SCHOLASTIC INC.

New York Toronto London Auckland Sydney
Mexico City New Delhi Hong Kong Buenos Aires

Developed by Nancy Hall, Inc.
Designed by R studio T
Photo research by Laura Miller

ISBN 0-439-31459-3

12 11 10 9 8 7 6 3 4 5 6 7 / 0

Printed in the U.S.A.
First Scholastic printing, March 2002

Contents

Ripley's
Believe It or Not!®

Amazing
Escapes

Introduction

Ripley's Amazing, Unpredictable World

Think of the most famous celebrity you know. Perhaps the name of a sports figure, movie star, or recording artist comes to mind. That's how famous Robert Ripley was in his time. In the 1930s and 1940s, the Believe It or Not! craze was so popular that the phrase "There's one for Rip" was on everyone's lips whenever they saw or heard of an incredible person, animal, or event.

Although Ripley was a world traveler, he did not have to go far for inspiration. He received more than 3,500 letters per day—that's a million letters per year—from people who hoped that one of their experiences would be amazing enough to be featured in a Believe It or Not! cartoon.

Though his fame made it possible for Robert Ripley to live a life that was wealthy, ordered, and secure, he was well aware that all of his good luck could vanish in an instant. His cartoons were filled with stories that demonstrated the unpredictability of life—tales about people struck by lightning on sunny days, of shark attacks in shallow waters, and of tornadoes roaring through in the night.

Robert Ripley once tried to buy Paricutín, the volcano that was born in a Mexican cornfield (*see page 13 and color insert*).

Catastrophic disasters could occur at any time, especially in coastal regions and near fault lines, rivers, and volcanoes. The earth might swallow a city, a storm could level structures that had taken years to build, and rampaging floods or torrents of boiling lava might reduce a home to a mound of rubble or smoldering ash at any moment. Ripley marveled at such terrible events.

But even more astonishing to him were the stories of the handful of survivors who, either by a stroke of good luck or by their own wits,

squeaked through such disasters unharmed.

In *Amazing Escapes*, you'll find all kinds of thrilling stories of survival and heroism from the Ripley's archives. You can also test your "stranger than fiction" smarts by taking the No Way! quizzes and solving the Brain Buster in each chapter. Then you can try the special Pop Quiz at the end of the book and use the scorecard to rank your Ripley's knowledge.

So get ready! You're about to discover the amazing variety of people and animals that have endured every imaginable form of disaster—and a few unimaginable ones as well.

Believe It!®

CHAPTER 1 Nature's Fury

The survivors on the following pages have braved tornadoes, floods, lightning bolts, earthquakes, volcanic eruptions, and more.

Rude Awakening: On May 8, 1905, Oliver Ellwin of Lindsborg, Kansas, was sound asleep when a tornado whirled through his bedroom, swept his bed out of the house, and set the bed—and Ellwin—down unharmed in a field 500 feet away.

The sound of the tornadoes in the movie *Twister* was made by a . . .

a. motorcycle in a tunnel.
b. pack of howling wolves.
c. subway train.
d. moaning camel.

Mud Bath: In 1997, Virginia Davidson took refuge in her bathtub and waited for a tornado to pass through her hometown of Jarrell, Texas. Before she knew it, she was swept into the air, then set down in a field, right in the middle of a mud puddle. The bathtub was nowhere in sight.

Record Breaker: A tornado that struck Eldorado, Kansas, in 1958 sucked a woman through a window, carried her 60 feet through the air, and dropped her unharmed next to a broken record of "Stormy Weather." The tornado then collapsed her house like a pack of cards.

Grounded: In 1953, several children were playing together when a tornado struck Worcester, Massachusetts. Caught in the whirlwind of the tornado, the children were suddenly whisked into the air. Luckily, their mothers were around to grab hold of the kids and drag them back to earth.

Homespun: During a winter storm, a cottage in Malagash Point, Canada, was lifted from its foundation and set down a quarter mile away. Amazingly, everything inside remained intact—even the bottles on top of a kitchen cabinet.

No Way!

Benjamin Franklin once tried to break up a tornado by . . .

a. chasing it on horseback and lashing at it with a whip.
b. swinging at it with a lighted torch.
c. throwing chunks of dry ice at it.
d. spraying it with a hose.

At the End of Their Rope: In 1893, a hurricane smashed into South Carolina. With high winds blowing away anything in its path, many fast-thinking residents saved their lives by tying themselves to sturdy trees.

Moving Experience: In Pennsylvania, a 12-room house was carried away by the Johnstown flood on May 31, 1889. It was deposited two miles away on a foundation laid for a house that was being built from *identical* blueprints by the same contractor. William Thomas, owner of the property, bought the house and lived there for 43 years.

No Way!

In ancient Rome, it was believed that storms were caused by . . .

a. angering the god Jupiter.
b. wearing a soiled toga.
c. sporting a bad haircut.
d. speaking ill of one's mother-in-law.

Whew! On March 23, 1989, an asteroid larger than an aircraft carrier, traveling at a speed of about 46,000 miles per hour missed Earth by only six hours—or about 430,000 miles.

Up on the Rooftop:

In 1986, cows that were caught in a raging flood in Kansas climbed up on the rooftops of submerged houses and stayed there until they were rescued.

Windfall: On October 9, 1992, a tremendous bang sent Michelle Knapp of Peekskill, New York, scurrying from her house to investigate. What she found was puzzling at first. The trunk of her car had been badly smashed, but there was no other car in sight. When Knapp looked under the car, she found a foul-smelling rock about the size of a watermelon. It was a meteorite that had crashed to Earth—and hit her car on the way. Knapp had paid only $100 for her 12-year-old Chevrolet Malibu, but collectors paid her $10,000 to get the car—and well over $50,000 to get the meteorite.

Lucky Strike: Eddie Robinson of Falmouth, Maine, was blind and partially deaf for nine years after suffering head injuries. In 1980, he was struck by lightning—and his vision and hearing were suddenly restored.

Branded! In 1968, a bolt of lightning tattooed a man with the initials of a doctor whom he had once robbed. Even more amazing, the man was revived by that very same doctor, who had just happened to be on the scene.

All Fired Up: After he was struck by lightning during a golf game, Anders B. Rasmussen of Denmark saw sparks shooting out of his fingers. To Rasmussen, the fact that he was still standing was a lucky sign, so he continued playing, hoping that his good luck would spill over to his game.

No Way!

A single bolt of lightning can produce 20,000 megawatts—enough energy to . . .

a. cool an entire sports arena.
b. fuel a space shuttle.
c. heat all the buildings in Manhattan.
d. supply all of Arizona with electricity.

Money to Burn:

In January of 1990, Canadians Don Wing and Jack Joneson got lost while skiing at Big Mountain Resort in Montana. They survived the extreme cold by burning dollar bills.

Suspended Sentence:

Mount Pelée, on the island of Martinique in the West Indies, erupted in 1902, killing more than 30,000 people and destroying the city of St. Pierre. Raoul Sarteret, a murderer who'd been sentenced to hang, was found in his dungeon-like jail cell, severely burned by the cloud of hot ash and gas but alive. Sarteret was later pardoned and went on to become a respected missionary.

The Candy Diet: James Scott of Brisbane, Australia, was lost in a blizzard in the Himalayas. He survived for 43 days with only two candy bars to sustain him.

No Way!

On August 27, 1883, the fiery volcanic explosion on Krakatoa, an island in Indonesia, was heard as far as 3,000 miles away. The first landing party to reach the ruined island found no survivors except for one . . .

a. ash-covered beetle.
b. red spider spinning its web.
c. cockroach crawling out of the ash.
d. dragonfly skimming an ashy puddle.

Hot Stuff! For weeks there were tremors and rumbling sounds near the village of Paricutín, Mexico. Then on February 20, 1943, while a farmer named Dionisio Pulido was burning brush in his cornfield, the ground swelled up and cracked open. Sulfurous gas and smoke poured out. By nightfall, the fissure was spitting hot cinders into the air. Within 24 hours, a cone had risen to 160 feet, and within a week, it had grown to more than 300 feet high. Named after the first of two villages it eventually covered with lava and ash, the new volcano, Paricutín, stood 1,100 feet above its base within a year.

Whatever Works! When Mauna Loa erupted in 1880, an ocean of molten lava crept down the mountainside for six months, covering an area larger than the state of Rhode Island. The flow halted just one half mile before reaching the city of Hilo, more than 30 miles away! Many Hawaiians claimed that Hilo was spared because the Princess Kamahamena had thrown a lock of her hair into the fiery mass, hoping to calm it. When Mauna Loa erupted in 1935, the 23rd Bomb Squadron of the U.S. Army used twenty 600-pound bombs to change the direction of the lava flow and once again save Hilo from destruction.

Rocking and Rolling: With little warning, Mayon erupted on July 26, 2001 (*see color insert*). The Philippine volcano blasted out rocks the size of cars and sent them rolling down its slopes at speeds of 60 miles per hour. More than 40,000 villagers were forced to flee their homes. Ash showers known as "black rain" fell on towns as far as 31 miles away, turning morning into night. Though the eruption caused untold property damage, not a single life was lost.

What a Blast! For several months, Mount Saint Helens, a volcano in the state of Washington, had been rumbling and smoking. On May 18, 1990, geologists Keith and Dorothy Stoffel took off in their small plane to get a bird's-eye view of the crater. As they got close to the peak, there was a huge explosion. The pilot dived steeply to gain speed and they were able to outrun the huge cloud of hot ash and make it to safety with some of the finest photographs they'd ever taken.

No Way!

The eruption of Mount Saint Helens created enough ash and dust to . . .

a. fill in the Grand Canyon.
b. cover all of Manhattan to a depth of 28 stories.
c. completely fill the Houston Astrodome.
d. cover the entire state of Rhode Island.

Slice of Life:
In December of 1920, earthquakes caused massive landslides in China. In one valley, three men survived when their farm split away from a cliff and traveled intact down the valley on a river of watery clay.

Jail Quakes:
Gabriel Maghalhaens (1609–1677), a Portuguese missionary to China, was arrested six times by Chinese authorities and received a death sentence all six times. On the night before each execution, however, an earthquake demolished his prison and set him free.

No Way!

Just before an earthquake struck the French Riviera in 1887 . . .

a. fish jumped out of the sea into boats.
b. all the cats began to meow at once.
c. horses refused to eat.
d. all the flowers wilted.

Fell Through the Crack: When the largest North American earthquake ever recorded struck Alaska in 1964, Balas Ervin looked out a window and saw the earth suddenly shoot up 50 feet. The house had plunged to the bottom of a crevasse. Cans from the cupboards rained down on Ervin and a maid as they ran for the back door. Once outside, they struggled to stay on their feet while the ground continued to shake. Finally, Ervin gave the maid a boost, and they clambered to the top of the fissure and escaped.

Road Trip: In 1920, a poplar-lined highway in China, was carried intact for nearly a mile by a landslide. Even the birds' eggs in their nests were entirely unharmed.

A River Runs Backward: In 1811 and 1812, a series of major earthquakes struck New Madrid, Missouri, and played havoc with nature. In one place, both banks of the Mississippi River caved in, forcing the water to flow upstream.

On Shaky Ground: During the New Madrid, Missouri, earthquakes, huge cracks appeared in the ground. Noticing that they all ran in the same direction, the residents cut down trees and laid them at right angles to the fissures, When the earth trembled again, the people leaped onto the tree trunks, hoping the logs would serve as bridges across any new cracks and keep them safe.

No Shock Value: A Los Angeles earthquake in 1971 knocked out the seismograph—an instrument that records vibrations in the earth—in nearby Pasadena. It was here that Charles Richter (1900–1985) developed the Richter Scale, which measures earthquake intensity, in the early 1930s.

On the Ball:

In A.D. 132, a Chinese inventor named Chang Heng (A.D. 78–c. 142) devised the world's first instrument to detect earthquakes—even if the tremors were too far away to be felt. Heng's seismoscope was about eight feet tall and shaped like an urn. Around the outside of the urn were eight dragons, each holding a ball in its mouth and facing in a different direction. Below them were eight frogs. Whenever there was an earthquake, the inner workings of the urn triggered one of the dragons to drop its ball into the mouth of the frog below it, making a clanging noise. One day, a ball dropped, but no one nearby felt even the slightest tremor. It wasn't until several days later that a messenger came with word that an earthquake had indeed struck Lung-Hsi, which was located 400 miles away!

No Way!

About five earthquakes a year result in the loss of life. Yet, each year earthquakes that cause only mild tremors number more than . . .

a. one thousand.
b. five hundred.
c. one hundred.
d. one million.

Wave Good-bye: In 1946, a Hawaiian family survived a tsunami, an enormous sea wave, that lifted their house off the foundation, swept it 200 feet, and deposited it in a cane field—with the family's breakfast still simmering on the stove.

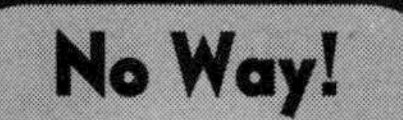

After one city was leveled by a tidal wave in the fall of 1900, it was raised 17 feet above sea level and totally rebuilt. The name of this city is . . .

a. Charleston, South Carolina.
b. Galveston, Texas.
c. Provincetown, Massachusetts.
d. Miami, Florida.

On Board: In 1868, Holoua, a resident of Kauai, Hawaii, whose home was swept out to sea by a tidal wave, saved himself by tearing a plank from the wall of the house and riding it back to shore. This event has been recorded in Honolulu as the highest wave ever surfed.

Ripley's Believe It or Not! Brain Buster

Ripley believed that fact is stranger than fiction. Do you? Get ready to test your ability to tell a mind-blowing true tale from flat-out fiction!

The Ripley files are packed with true stories of daring deeds, unfortunate events, survivor skills, and close calls.

Each Believe It or Not! Brain Buster contains a group of four shockingly strange statements. In each group only **one** is **false**. Read each extraordinary entry and circle whether you **Believe It!** or **Not!** If you survive the challenge, take on the bonus question in each section and the bonus round at the end of the book. Then flip to the answer key, keep track of your score, and rate your skills. Got it? Good. Here goes . . .

Many athletes face extreme conditions on a regular basis—and completely by choice. Sports can be dangerous, but these adventurers came out on top. Only one of these extreme exploits is erroneous. Can you figure out which one?

a. Bicycle marathons are tough. So tough that Bobby Walthour was pronounced dead twice during one 60-day race. He recovered both times and peddled on.

Believe It! **Not!**

b. Tao Berman was the first person to paddle a kayak over Johnston Canyon Waterfall in Alberta, Canada. Lined on both sides with jagged rock, the 98-foot drop is as high as a ten-story building.

Believe It! **Not!**

c. Eighteen-year-old Regina Nair became a legend when she snowboarded down an icy peak near Mount Everest. Though she fell and broke her leg near the peak, Nair kept on and made it to the base, setting a new record.

Believe It! **Not!**

d. Wim Hof of Holland dove into a hole carved through two feet of ice and swam 164 feet in one minute and six seconds. The kicker? The water was only two degrees warmer than the water that *Titanic* passengers froze in.

Believe It! **Not!**

BONUS QUESTION

How did Wilma Rudolph of Clarksville, Tennessee, show the world that she's a survivor?

a. At 103, she was the oldest person ever to complete a marathon, running more than 26 miles.

b. She won three gold medals for running in the 1960 Olympics even though she had suffered from polio—a life-threatening illness—and worn leg braces as a child.

c. She went on to win a skateboarding competition just five minutes after she was struck by lightning.

Chapter 2 Littlest Escape Artists

Kids and animals get into scrapes sometimes. What's truly amazing is how often they get out of them.

No Yolk! In 1947, two-year-old baby Zsuzsie of Yugoslavia fell from a third-story window and landed in a basket of eggs carried by a passing peasant woman. The baby was not hurt—but the eggs got a little scrambled.

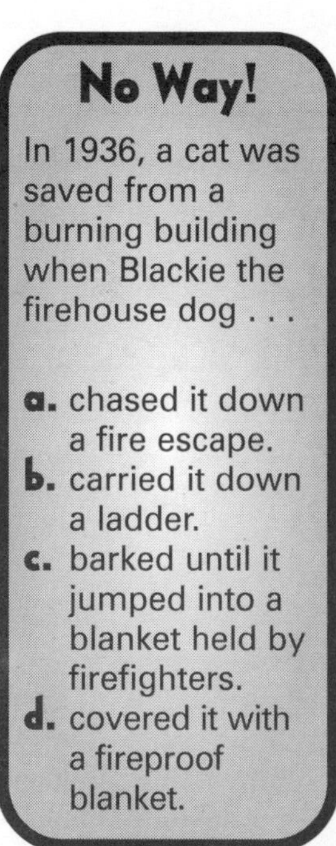

No Way!

In 1936, a cat was saved from a burning building when Blackie the firehouse dog . . .

a. chased it down a fire escape.
b. carried it down a ladder.
c. barked until it jumped into a blanket held by firefighters.
d. covered it with a fireproof blanket.

Rock-a-Bye Baby . . . In 1889, the flood that wiped out Johnstown, Pennsylvania, killed thousands. But it spared one five-month-old infant who sailed all the way to Pittsburgh, 75 miles away, on the floorboards of a ruined house.

. . . on the Treetop: After a tornado swept through Marshfield, Missouri, in April 1880, a baby girl was found sleeping peacefully in the branches of a tall elm tree.

Little Dropout: In 1992, Joshua Beatty, age two, of Southfield, Michigan, fell from a ninth-floor window. Incredibly, he survived unharmed. Why? Because the edge of his diaper got snagged on a bush, breaking his fall.

Happy Endings

Made a Big Splash: In 1996, when a shark attacked Martin Richardson in the Red Sea, a few dolphins slapped the water with their fins and tails to keep the shark away until Richardson could be rescued.

What a Pig! When Jo Altsman had a heart attack, her pet pig, Lulu, squeezed through a doggie door and ran out into the street. There she lay down and played dead to attract help—and ultimately saved her owner's life.

One Great Ape: A silverback gorilla named Jambo came to the rescue when five-year-old Levan Merritt fell into the gorilla compound in England's Jersey Zoo, keeping the other gorillas away while comforting the boy until help arrived.

Wreck and Ruin

Hail and Hearty:
A pilot flew his biplane 275 miles and landed safely—after it was riddled with 4,700 holes made by hailstones the size of baseballs!

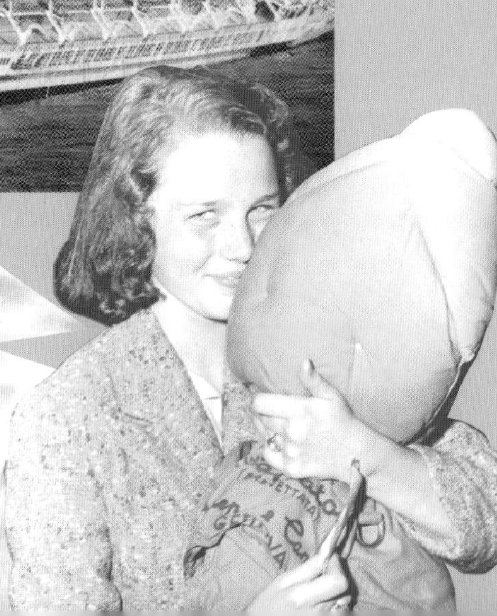

One Foggy Night:
Ann MacKenzie hugged her lifejacket after learning that her mother was also among the 1,654 passengers who were rescued after the *Andrea Doria* (above) and the MV *Stockholm* collided in the North Atlantic.

Good Timing: In 1993, all 163 passengers on an Air India flight that crashed and landed upside down walked away from the wreckage before the plane burst into flames.

Bad Timing: Seconds after a car slid down an embankment onto the railroad tracks in Selby, England, a passenger train carrying about 100 people and traveling at 125 miles per hour crashed into it. The train then hit an oncoming freight train carrying 1,000 tons of coal. Miraculously, only ten people lost their lives.

ON SHAKY GROUND

Into the Abyss: When an earthquake struck Alaska in 1964, the house where Balas Ervin was working plunged to the bottom of a crevasse. Ervin escaped, surviving the largest North American earthquake ever recorded.

Swept Away: Nine-year-old Hilda Degaway was found dazed but alive in a swamp miles from home, four days after huge tidal waves swept her away from her village in Papua New Guinea.

"Miracle of Valzur": Four-year-old Alexander Walter survived being buried in the snow for almost two hours after an avalanche covered his house in the Alpine village of Valzur, Austria.

Sole Survivor: In 1997, sixty-five hours after a landslide buried two ski lodges in Thredbo, Australia, rescuers pulled ski instructor Stuart Diver from the rubble. He was the only survivor.

Buried Alive! When heavy rains sent rivers of mud down the mountainsides of Sarno, Italy, Roberto Robustelli was trapped for three days beneath tons of dirt and debris. He survived with only minor injuries.

They Blew Their Stacks

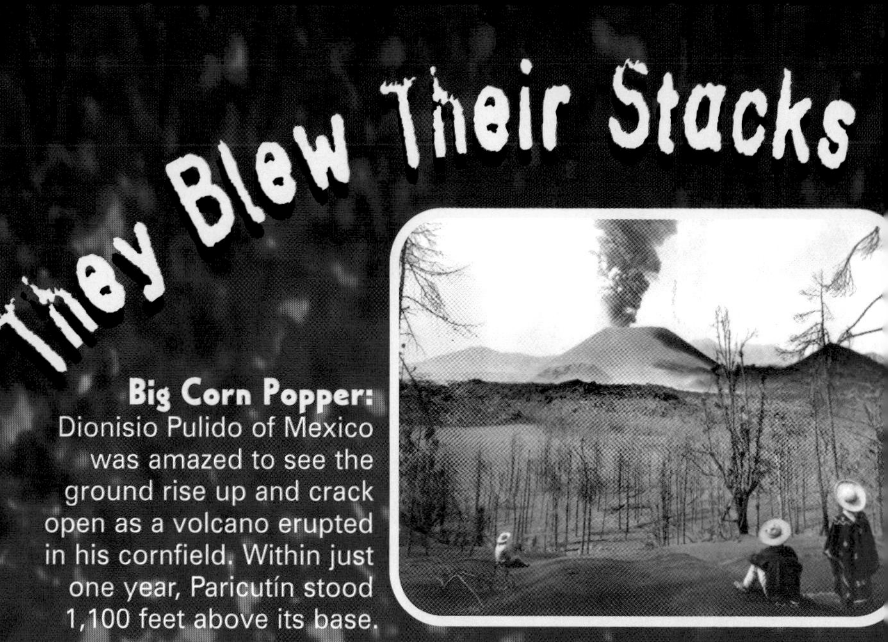

Big Corn Popper: Dionisio Pulido of Mexico was amazed to see the ground rise up and crack open as a volcano erupted in his cornfield. Within just one year, Paricutín stood 1,100 feet above its base.

Bombs Away! In 1935, the 23rd Bomb Squadron dropped twenty 600-pound bombs on the lava flowing from Mauna Loa, diverting the flow and saving the city of Hilo from destruction.

A Rain of Fire: Mount Pelée erupted in 1902, wiping out the city of St. Pierre, Martinique. Four days later, a convicted murderer named Raoul Sarteret was found in his cell, severely burned but alive.

Blasting Off: When Mayon erupted in the Philippines, sending a fiery avalanche speeding down its slopes at over 60 miles per hour, more than 40,000 people fled. Amazingly, not one person died.

Hot Stuff: Seconds after Mount Saint Helens exploded in May 1980, Jim Scymanky, a logger working ten miles away, was engulfed by a cloud of red-hot ash. Though badly burned, he was the only one of his crew to survive.

Burned Up:
In 1871, Chicago was a city of 330,000 people. When fire raged through the city, destroying more than 17,000 buildings and leaving nearly 100,000 people homeless, all but 250 people miraculously survived.

Heartwarming:
After a washing machine exploded in Nottingham, England, in June 2001, a pet hamster was overcome by smoke. His life was saved when a firefighter gave him oxygen and a one-finger heart massage.

Birdbrain:
When fire blazed through Ye Olde Cheshire Cheese Pub in Derbyshire, England, Henry the parrot squawked "Hello" until a firefighter rescued him.

Blackened Fish:
Twenty-six people landed in the hospital after the sun shining through a glass gold-fish bowl started a fire in Oxford, England. The people survived. The goldfish did not.

Bumper Sticker:
In 1993, two-year-old Allyson Hoary's dad got into his van to run an errand. Little did he know that Allyson was climbing on the back of the van as if it were a jungle gym at the time. He had already traveled six miles at 60 miles per hour when another motorist alerted him to the problem.

When Hoary pulled over, he found Allyson clinging to the back of the van, shaken but uninjured.

No Way!

In 1993, five-year-old Paul Rosen of New York City lived after falling . . .

a. out of a taxi going 40 miles per hour.
b. off the Brooklyn Bridge.
c. from a seven-story apartment building.
d. through a grate onto the subway platform 25 feet below.

Lucky PJs: At the age of two, Albert Joseph of Miramar, Florida, fell into an unfenced canal bordering his backyard. He was saved from drowning when his pajamas filled with air, keeping little Albert's head above water.

Web Site: On July 13, 2001, a mama duck waddled up to a police officer in downtown Vancouver, Canada, and grabbed hold of his pant leg. Officer Ray Peterson pulled away from her, but she continued to quack and peck at him. Finally catching on, Peterson followed the duck to a sewer grate where he saw eight ducklings swimming in the water below. A tow truck was called, the heavy metal grate was lifted, and the mama's babies were pulled to safety in a colander.

Buried Alive: Glenda Stevens was heartbroken when her small black dog, Sweetie, was hit by a mail truck. She listened carefully for a heartbeat. When she didn't hear one, she tearfully buried her beloved pet in her backyard. Hours later, Stevens saw Sweetie's hind legs sticking out of the ground. Sweetie, who wasn't dead after all, was digging herself out!

Not Too Sharp: In 1993, Tyro, a three-month-old Labrador retriever puppy in British Columbia, Canada, made a full recovery after swallowing a nine-inch knife!

Blackout: In 1997, Sparky, a black cat in East Corinth, Maine, was trapped for three days on top of a telephone pole. The cat survived thunderstorms and a jolt from a 7,500-volt power line that had left 1,000 homes without electricity.

No Way!

Nathan King, age 12, of Helena, Montana, made a full recovery after an accident on March 8, 2000, in which he . . .

a. lunged for a football and landed on a pencil that pierced his heart.
b. fell from a plane without a parachute.
c. fell off a deck into an empty swimming pool.
d. stumbled off a stage and fell into the orchestra pit.

Eggs-tremely Resourceful: A red hen owned by J. D. Rucker was trapped in a crate when a tornado devastated the town of Gainesville, Georgia. It was rescued 47 days later on May 22, 1936. Noticeably thinner, it had survived by eating its own eggs.

Barn-Sided: In 1998, Kate Wilson of London, England, got out of her car, leaving her two dogs inside. The romping canines accidentally released the emergency brake—and took an unexpected joyride that lasted until they crashed into the side of a barn.

Go Fly a Kite: Eight-year-old Deandra Anrig was flying her brand-new 12-foot-wide kite at Shoreline Park in Mountain View, California, when all of a sudden, a twin-engine plane caught the kite's nylon line. The plane lifted the little girl off the ground and carried her 100 feet before she let go—just in time to avoid smashing into a very large tree.

Taken by Storm: In 1908, 18-month-old Renée Nivernas of France was kidnapped and held for ransom aboard a boat. When a storm blew up, the boat sank and all eight kidnappers drowned. But Renée, asleep in a packing-case cradle, floated ashore unharmed.

No Way!

In 1993, eight-year-old Nicole Bernier of Willington, Connecticut, survived after . . .

a. falling out the window of her third-floor bedroom.
b. spending two days beneath an avalanche.
c. a freight train passed over her body.
d. she fell to the bottom of the Grand Canyon.

Way Down Under: In 1990, nine-month-old Sara Gillies, of Perth, Australia, survived after her baby carriage was hit and crushed by an oncoming train.

Trial by Fire: In 1947, when Albert Lametta was 12 years old, he climbed to the top of an electrical tower, touched a 6,600-volt wire, and fell 60 feet. Though badly burned, he eventually made a full recovery.

Fish Tale: In July of 1999, a goldfish was scooped from a pond by a heron and dropped down a chimney in Northampton, England—where it bounced off the hot coals before it was rescued and placed in a bowl of water.

Where's Toto? In 1994, a tornado in Le Mars, Iowa, picked up a doghouse with a dog inside and set it down several blocks away without harming the dog in any way.

No Way!

On September 8, 1860, 297 lives were lost when the *Lady Elgin* sank in Lake Michigan. One little boy, Charles Beverung, saved himself by . . .

a. clinging to the coffin of a dead man.
b. using his drum as a life raft.
c. jumping off the deck onto a steamer trunk.
d. treading water for 14 hours.

Home Wrecker: Five-month-old James Clark of West Bend, Wisconsin, was sound asleep when a tornado blew his room apart and dropped him outside on the sidewalk. The baby was not injured!

Bolt Out of the Blue: On a beautiful sunny day in June 2001, a Little Leaguer in North Carolina was covering third base when a sudden storm blew in. There was a sound like a cannon shot, and the boy was struck by a bolt of lightning. Luckily, he was revived on the field and rushed to the hospital, where he was treated for burns.

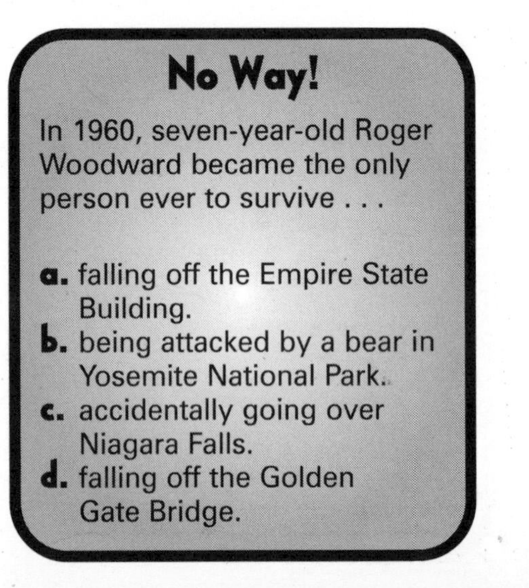

No Way!

In 1960, seven-year-old Roger Woodward became the only person ever to survive . . .

a. falling off the Empire State Building.
b. being attacked by a bear in Yosemite National Park.
c. accidentally going over Niagara Falls.
d. falling off the Golden Gate Bridge.

Life is filled with narrow escapes and near misses—some more dramatic than others. Three of the following escapes are 100% accurate, but one is totally made up. Can you pick out the fiction?

a. In 1997, Nigel Etherington of Perth, Australia, rescued a baby kangaroo. The kangeroo later returned the favor when it woke Etherington up during a fire by banging its tail on a door.

Believe It! **Not!**

b. In 1775, three women in a ruined stable in Stura Valley, Italy, survived being buried by a 60-foot-deep avalanche of snow. But they didn't escape unscathed. When the women were rescued, one had lost all of her hair and another could no longer speak.

Believe It! **Not!**

c. The small South American island of Tristan da Cunha is the only place on Earth that escaped the 1918 Spanish influenza—a fast-spreading disease that killed more than 21 million people all over the world.

Believe It! **Not!**

d. In July 2000, a 12-year-old girl accidentally fell into a raging river near her family's home and was quickly swept downstream by the current. The girl was seconds away from crashing into a giant boulder when a female black bear jumped into the water, swam the girl to shore, and left her on the ground unharmed.

Believe It! **Not!**

BONUS QUESTION

How did King Malcolm McAnmore of Scotland's bodyguard keep 20 assassins from killing the king?

a. By triggering an avalanche. The bodyguard fired off a cannon on the roof of the castle, which sent 40 tons of snow and ice tumbling onto the assassins below.

b. By holding the castle door closed with just one arm and preventing the assassins from getting in.

c. By firing a cannon into the moat surrounding the castle. The water rose, drowning a few of the assassins and distracting the others long enough for the bodyguard and the king to sneak out of the castle through a secret underground passage.

CHAPTER 3 Rudders, Wheels, and Wings

Transportation mishaps can be deadly—one wrong move, and you're history. What's unbelievable is that so many people survive!

Crushing Experience:

In 1994, a truck in Arenys de Mar, Spain, was hit by a car, pushed onto a railroad track, and crushed by an oncoming train. The truck's driver and passenger walked away from the wreck with only minor injuries.

No Way!

In 1999, British actress Sara Donohue survived a crash at 100 miles per hour while racing her . . .

a. boat.
b. motorcycle.
c. Formula 1 race car.
d. snowmobile.

Stone-Walled: A biplane caught in a storm flew 275 miles from Colorado to Oklahoma with 4,700 holes in its wings and fuselage. What made so many holes? Hailstones the size of baseballs!

The Whole Scoop: In 1955, the drivers of two cars that collided in Santa Barbara, California, walked away uninjured. One was named Coffey and the other Pott, but the police found no *grounds* on which to hold either driver.

No Way!

The ship *Californian* was only five miles away from the sinking *Titanic,* but instead of coming to its aid, the captain calmly went to sleep after . . .

a. turning off the ship's radio and missing the SOS call.
b. misreading a chart and thinking the *Titanic* was 500 miles away.
c. his radio operator fell asleep and missed the call for help.
d. he mistook the *Titanic*'s emergency flares for fireworks.

Take a Dive:

After colliding with another skydiver near Phoenix, Arizona, in April 1987, Debbie Williams was knocked unconscious. It's a good thing Gregory Robertson was the next person to jump. He caught up to her by going into a 200-mile-per-hour free fall and opened her parachute just seconds before she would have struck the ground.

Busch-Whacked:

In 1953, a car driven by Clayton Busch was hit by two trains at the same time. Busch was found standing close to the tracks, still clutching the car's steering wheel.

Under-Tow: Because motorists' cars frequently plunge into Amsterdam's many canals, drivers in the city are given courses in how to get themselves out of automobiles that are submerged in water.

Charmed Life: Frank Tower swam away from three major shipwrecks: the *Titanic* in 1912, the *Empress of Ireland* in 1914, and the *Lusitania* in 1915.

On the Beam: During a violent storm in the 19th century, Captain Benjamin Webster was swept overboard from the *Isaac Johnson* at the same time that a load of lumber on deck was cut loose. The captain landed on one of the beams. A moment later, a giant wave hurled that *one* board back onto the ship's deck with the captain safely astride it.

Springing to Life: After the shipwrecked *Lara* was destroyed by fire in 1881, its crew drifted for 23 days in three lifeboats off the coast of Mexico. Several crewmen were unconscious from thirst. But they were saved when the captain noticed that the water beneath their boats had changed color from blue to green as they drifted over a freshwater spring. The fresh water revived them, and the entire crew reached Mexico safely.

No Way!

A jetliner was delayed in Juneau, Alaska, for an hour after a midair mishap caused by . . .

a. hailstones that damaged the fuselage.
b. a seagull that flew into the engine.
c. a salmon (that was dropped by an eagle) crashing through the windshield.
d. a family of geese that hitched a ride on a wing.

One Foggy Night: On July 25, 1956, two passenger ships, the *Andrea Doria* and the *MV Stockholm* crashed in the North Atlantic near Nantucket, Massachusetts. Survivors remember feeling a massive jolt and hearing the sickening noise of crunching metal. Though 46 passengers died that foggy night, the incident remains one of the most amazing rescues in the history of maritime disasters. The rest of the 1,654 passengers were pulled to safety aboard the five ships that answered the distress call. Coincidentally, one of the survivors, Ruby MacKenzie, had just finished reading *A Night to Remember,* a novel about the sinking of the *Titanic.*

The Right Wavelength: In May 1945, Lieutenant Commander Robert W. Goehring was swept off his ship by a mountainous wave during a storm. Just when he thought that all was lost, another giant wave tossed him back on board to safety.

Stress Test: On July 19, 2001, a teenager was passing her driving test with flying colors—until she attempted to parallel park. Somehow she lost control of the car, smashed into four other cars, then spun around and hit two more. The driving instructor was treated for shock, and the teen and a woman who was standing between two of the cars had minor injuries, but no one was seriously hurt.

In Nantucket, Massachusetts, lumber salvaged from shipwrecks was used to build a . . .

a. tavern.
b. windmill.
c. captain's home.
d. lighthouse.

In a Tailspin: On a routine passenger flight over Czechoslovakia in 1972, flight attendant Vesna Vulovic was inside the plane's tail when the plane exploded. She survived being thrown 33,000 feet to the ground.

Narrow Escape: In 1993, all 163 passengers on an Air India flight that crashed and landed *upside down* walked away from the wreckage before the plane burst into flames. (*See color insert.*)

Icebound: When their ship, the *Endurance,* became icebound in 1914, Ernest Shackleton and his entire 27-man crew survived 19 months of brutal weather and dangerous travel across Antartica's ice and frigid waters.

Tall Tail: Captain J. H. Hedley of Chicago, Illinois, fell out of a plane nearly three miles up in the air on January 6, 1918. Incredibly, just as the plane was making a steep vertical dive in line with his own fall, Hedley landed on the tail. He made it to the ground, shaken but uninjured.

All Clogged Up: When ash from a volanic eruption in Alaska clogged and stalled the engines of a Dutch passenger plane in 1989, the airliner went into a dive and plunged two miles. To the relief of everyone aboard, the pilots were able to get the engines started again and safely land the plane.

No Way!

After the *Titanic* sank, most newspapers carried a headline announcing that . . .

a. there were no survivors.
b. everyone had been rescued.
c. the captain had been saved.
d. the ship was being towed to shore.

Piggyback Landing: In December of 1999, flight instructor Alan Vangee was flying with student Barbara Yeninas in a Cessna 152 when a Piper Cadet airplane cleared to land on the same runway wedged itself on top of their plane. Vangee successfully landed the two planes—and no one was hurt.

No Way!

In a study of over 260 voice-recorder tapes removed from airplanes involved in accidents since 1966, 80 percent revealed that during the last half hour of flight, one of the pilots was . . .

a. phoning his wife.
b. laughing at a joke.
c. whistling.
d. gossiping with a flight attendant.

The Ripley's files are filled with some very bizarre accounts of near tragedy. Which of these amazing escapes is completely false?

a. In 1989, Buster Bradshaw of Haverford, Pennsylvania, survived the crash of his private plane by holding a wheel of Swiss cheese over his face. The soft cheese cushioned the impact and prevented Bradshaw from suffering severe injuries to the head.

Believe It! **Not!**

b. In 1985, Eric Villet of Orléans, France, was pronounced officially dead after doctors unsuccessfully tried to revive him with heart massage and oxygen. Shockingly, he started breathing on his own three days later—while lying in the morgue!

Believe It! **Not!**

c. During the World Extreme Skiing Championship in 1992, Garret Bartelt tumbled down the mountain's steepest slope without protective gear. It was the longest fall in professional skiing history—but Bartelt survived with only minor injuries and was back on the slopes competing in another championship two years later.

Believe It! **Not!**

d. In the 1930s, Douglas Ellis of Cleveland, Ohio, came in contact with a 22,000-volt line. Although 60 square inches of his skull were removed, Ellis survived.

Believe It! **Not!**

BONUS QUESTION

How did Admiral Richard E. Byrd survive temperatures of 83°F *below* zero while spending six months in Antarctica?

a. By living in a 9-by-13-foot shack beneath the snow.

b. By burning the lining of his shoes to keep warm.

c. By exercising for 14 hours a day to keep his body temperature high.

Chapter 4 Nice Saves

Should you find yourself in a really tight spot, it's nice to know that there just might be someone brave enough to come to the rescue.

Track Star: On June 25, 1913, a locomotive on its way to Holland plunged over the side of a bridge. The engine, on the brink of falling, would have exploded if it were not for the engineer, who at great risk to himself climbed down through the engine to put out the fire in the furnace.

No Way!

A woman who fell down and lost consciousness was saved when a family pet went straight to her sister's house and tapped on the window. The pet was a . . .

a. goat.
b. collie.
c. canary.
d. pig.

In the Driver's Seat: In December of 1991, after the driver of his school bus blacked out, 12-year-old Kenny Perrone of Dunellon, Florida, came to the rescue. Quickly taking control of the wheel, he guided the vehicle to safety, saving all 33 kids on board.

Hangin' Eight: After a yacht capsized in rough waters off Newport Beach, California, in 1925, Hawaiian surfer Duke Kahanamoku single-handedly saved the lives of eight passengers by using his surfboard to carry them to shore.

Human Anchor: On October 28, 1844, Margaret Whyte of Aberdour, Scotland, was the only person onshore when the sailing ship *William Hope* was driven into the rocks by a raging storm. Whyte signaled the crew to throw her a line. With no tree or post available, she tied the rope around her waist, dug her heels into the sand, and held the line taut against the pull of the tossing vessel while its entire crew of 12 came ashore one by one.

No Way!

On September 22, 1938, hundreds of acres of valuable land in the town of Stony Point, New York, were saved from flooding by . . .

a. hundreds of trees felled by Eagle Scouts to divert the flow of water.
b. thousands of sandbags filled by townspeople.
c. the dams built by 60 beaver colonies.
d. tons of sludge dumped by the Coast Guard.

Critter Comfort: When five-year-old Levan Merritt fell 20 feet into a gorilla compound at England's Jersey Zoo, a gorilla named Jambo protected the injured boy by keeping the other gorillas away. Jambo then comforted the boy until human help could arrive.

Human Bus Stop: In December of 1996, bus driver Hamdija Osmana of Yugoslavia kept his bus from rolling over a cliff—with 30 passengers inside—by jamming his legs under a wheel and stopping the vehicle. He saved the lives of all 30 passengers.

Four to the Rescue: If it weren't for four brave siblings, three of their neighbors might have died in the fire that blazed through their Freeport, New York, home on July 16, 2001. Felicia Pettus was trapped in an upstairs room with her two young children, Alexis and Kyra. Responding to her screams, 14-year-old Robert Hester and 16-year-old Jacob ran into the house, braving smoke and rising flames. But when they got upstairs, they couldn't get the door open. The boys ran back outside, where their 12-year-old sister, Jaquana, and 17-year-old stepbrother, Nathaniel Richardson, were shouting encouragement. Urging Pettus to jump, the siblings caught Alexis, then her mother. Robert then ran back into the house to get Kyra. He emerged holding his shirt over his head with one arm and the toddler in the other. When firefighters arrived at the scene, they had nothing but praise for this family of young heroes.

No Way!

Count Felix von Luckener, a German cabin boy aboard the *Noibe,* fell overboard, but was kept afloat and saved from drowning by . . .

a. a sea turtle.
b. an albatross.
c. a dolphin.
d. a manatee.

Warm and Fuzzy Heating Pad: Accompanied by his dog Sheena, three-year-old Justin Pasero of Susanville, California, wandered away into the Sierra Nevada Mountains and spent the night inside a hollow log. He was kept from freezing to death by Sheena, who kept Justin warm with her own body.

This Little Piggy Played Dead: In Beaver Falls, Pennsylvania, a potbelly pig named Lulu saved the life of her owner. Jo Altsman was home alone the morning she suffered a massive heart attack. When she fell to the floor, Lulu lay her head on Altsman's chest and cried real tears. Then the brave pig sprang into action. Lulu squeezed herself through the doggie door, which was only one foot wide. Then she ran into the road where she lay down and played dead to get someone's attention. Minutes later, a young man stopped. Lulu got up and led the man to the trailer. When he knocked on the door, Altsman answered faintly, "Call 911." At the hospital, doctors credited Lulu with saving Altsman's life. (*See color insert.*)

Up in Arms: When fire ravaged a Milwaukee hotel in 1883, firefighter Van Haag fought the flames to save General Tom Thumb and his wife. Thumb, who was only three feet four inches tall, was a world-famous performer who worked for showman P. T. Barnum.

No Way!

During the 1800s, shipwrecked sailors sent lifelines to rescuers on shore by attaching them to . . .

a. seagulls.
b. kites.
c. fishing poles.
d. dolphins.

Pod Squad: In 1991, a pod of dolphins protected a group of shipwrecked sailors from circling sharks off the coast of Florida.

Did Swimmingly: Nellie O'Donnell had never learned to swim. But in June of 1904, she saw an excursion boat, the *General Slocum,* sinking in New York's East River. Hundreds of people were about to drown. With no thought for her own safety, O'Donnell jumped into the water and saved ten lives before she collapsed with exhaustion.

In a Heartbeat: In June 2001, a pet hamster was overcome by smoke after a washer exploded and started a fire in Nottingham, England. A firefighter saved the hamster's life by giving him oxygen and a one-finger heart massage. (*See color insert.*)

Nice Catch! Nine-year-old Joey Rains of Newark, California, caught 17-month-old Sara Wolf when she fell from an open second-story window of her apartment building. Neither was hurt.

Oh, Deer!

In 1992, Gene Chaffin of Encinitas, California, rescued a pregnant doe after she was struck by a car. He delivered her two fawns and saved one of them by giving it mouth-to-mouth resuscitation.

Human Cork: In January of 1870, Captain Thomas A. Scott brought his tugboat alongside a sinking ferryboat carrying hundreds of passengers in New York's North River. Boarding the ferry, Scott used his body to plug a hole at the waterline of the listing boat. His arm, which protruded through the hole, was severely lacerated by ice, but everyone aboard the vessel was saved.

No Way!

A short circuit caused a fire in the home of James A. Dewitt, who was saved when . . .

a. the short circuit set off the doorbell, jarring him awake.
b. his parrot kept squawking, "Get up, get up!"
c. a pipe burst and put out the fire.
d. his ferret crawled up his pajama leg and woke him up.

Canine Lifeline: On December 10, 1919, the S.S. *Ethie*, a 414-ton steamship, ran aground off Newfoundland, Canada, in a violent storm. With the ship breaking up in heavy seas, the captain couldn't launch the lifeboats, and none of the crew dared swim ashore with a lifeline. But all was not lost. A Newfoundland dog gripped the lifeline in his teeth and swam to the beach, where a bystander secured the line and all 92 passengers and crew were pulled to safety.

No Way!

In 1997, Gail Brooks's boyfriend was attacked by a shark. She saved his life by . . .

a. pouring sand into the wound to soak up the blood.
b. making a tourniquet out of her bathing suit strap.
c. tying off a bleeding artery with dental floss.
d. freezing the wound with ice from the cooler.

People will do the oddest things no matter how dangerous, terrifying, or life-threatening their actions may be. See if you can tell which one of these death-defying feats are false.

a. Tim Cridland takes performance art to a new height. Using only pain-deadening meditation, he lies down on a bed of nails and lets a 3,000-pound vehicle drive over him, surviving despite the huge weight and sharp nails.

Believe It! **Not!**

b. Sixteen-year-old Janice Stellman dived from a 500-foot cliff into the ocean off the coast of New Zealand in 1997 "just for fun." Stellman survived despite blacking out halfway down.

Believe It! **Not!**

c. In 1837, to demonstrate the power of meditation, yogi Haridas put himself into a trance, then allowed assistants to fill his ears, nose, and mouth with wax. The assistants went on to wrap him in a blanket and bury him alive. Forty days later, he was dug up, looking a little on the skinny side but perfectly healthy.

Believe It! **Not!**

d. Smokey Harris had his nose broken seven times, his jaw broken four times, his ribs broken 14 times, both knees broken, half a foot amputated, and 100 operations on his head—all for the sake of playing hockey. What dedication!

Believe It! **Not!**

BONUS QUESTION

Maddie Mix of Baton Rouge, Louisiana, is one lucky woman. She was driving in her car when nearly 10,000 bees attacked. How did she escape?

a. She happened to be eating a peanut butter and honey sandwich, which she used to distract the hungry bees while she carefully pulled over and slipped out of the car.

b. She drove her car through the wall of a nearby molasses silo, causing the sticky liquid to flow into the car and smother the bees.

c. She drove into a car wash where she was rescued by a beekeeper who just happened to be washing his car at the time.

If you think the escapes in the previous pages are unbelievable, wait until you read these!

Snake Medicine: In 1996, Valentin Grimald of Texas was bitten by a coral snake. He killed the poisonous reptile by biting off its head, then used its body as a tourniquet to stop the poison from spreading throughout his body, and saved his own life.

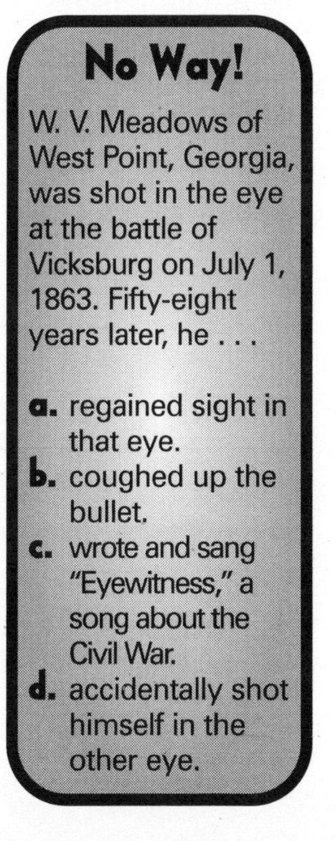

No Way!

W. V. Meadows of West Point, Georgia, was shot in the eye at the battle of Vicksburg on July 1, 1863. Fifty-eight years later, he . . .

a. regained sight in that eye.
b. coughed up the bullet.
c. wrote and sang "Eyewitness," a song about the Civil War.
d. accidentally shot himself in the other eye.

Saved by the Dill: In 1994, four restaurant employees in Jeffersonville, Indiana, were locked in a freezer by robbers, who then set fire to the building in an effort to destroy evidence. The fire was contained, however, when the blaze reached a plastic bucket of pickles. The bucket melted, the pickle juice extinguished the flames, and the victims were saved.

Tongue-Tied: Fourteen-year-old Duane Della of Altoona, Pennsylvania, reached out to grab his two-year-old niece who was climbing into the basement freezer. Unfortunately, Duane lost his balance and toppled in, landing face-first. When he opened his mouth to yell for help, his tongue instantly stuck fast to the bottom of the freezer. Fortunately, firefighters were able to loosen his tongue (from the freezer!) and pull him out.

Whale of a Story: In 1891, James Bartley, a 36-year-old seaman on the British whaler *Star of the East,* was swallowed by a sperm whale. Bartley's crewmates quickly harpooned the whale, badly injuring it. The next day, the whale was found dead, floating on the surface. After hauling it aboard and slicing it open, the crew found Bartley, unconscious but still breathing, in the whale's stomach. He was delirious for days but recovered to describe his ordeal. Before passing out, Bartley remembered seeing "a big ribbed canopy of light pink and white" above him, "a wall of soft flesh surrounding him and hemming him in," and then finding himself inside a water-filled sack among fish, some of which were still alive.

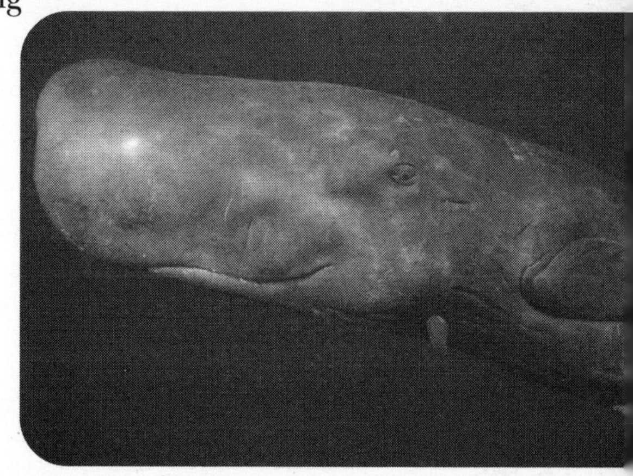

Snail's Pace: in 1996, a train on the Casablanca-Fez railroad line in Morocco slipped off the rails after a horde of snails slimed the tracks!

No Way!

In 1930, Phineas P. Gage of Cavendish, Vermont, survived an explosion that drove a 13-pound iron bar through his . . .

a. brain.
b. lungs.
c. heart.
d. stomach.

Blasted Sky-High: A blast of air pressure in 1905 blew Richard Creedon, a New York City sandhog (a person who works on tunnels for city waterlines), out of an East River tunnel shaft. Unhurt after flying through 27 feet of silt and water into the air, Creedon said, "Before I came down, I had a fine view of the city."

Cushy Landing: On January 6, 1983, Keung Ng of Boston, Massachusetts, was asleep in his fourth-floor apartment when the building was destroyed by an explosion. Incredibly, Ng survived. Still in his bed, he fell down three flights to where the ground floor used to be and landed on a pile of debris. Then Ng got up and walked away.

Horse Nonsense: During the Civil War, southern raiders kidnapped two slaves, a mother and her infant son, in Missouri. Mary disappeared, but her son was found and ransomed by his master for a valuable racehorse. Moses Carver then adopted the baby, who grew up to be the distinguished scientist and dean of Tuskegee Institute, George Washington Carver.

Such a Headache: In 1867, William Thompson of Omaha, Nebraska, was shot by Native Americans of the Cheyenne tribe. Thinking he was dead, they removed part of his scalp. Imagine their surprise when Thompson regained consciousness, grabbed his scalp, and ran. He later donated the scalp to the Omaha Public Library.

No Way!

Sarah Ann Henley survived falling 250 feet from the Clifton Suspension Bridge in England when . . .

a. her petticoat opened like a parachute.
b. an eagle swooped down and caught her dress in its beak.
c. she landed in the swimming pool of a yacht.
d. her dress caught on a steel girder.

Instant Weight Loss: Imprisoned for 100 days in the Tower of London, Sir Thomas Overbury (1581–1613) survived being fed a diet of nitric acid, hemlock, and ground diamonds.

Don't Mess with Me! In 1992, while diving off Catalina Island in California, Norma Hansen survived an attack by a great white shark by kicking its teeth out with her steel-toed boots.

Sealed with a Kiss: Downy Ferrer of Laguna Hills, California, had to be rescued by paramedics after she kissed her pet turtle. Why? Because it clamped onto her upper lip and wouldn't let go!

Balloonatic: In 1982, Larry Walters of California attached more than 40 weather balloons to his lawn chair and filled them with helium. He packed a soda, a two-way radio, and a pellet gun, then strapped himself to the chair. The rope holding the chair down was cut free—and Walters shot up three miles into the sky, where he drifted for hours before he got chilly, shot some of the balloons with his pellet gun, and drifted back to Earth.

No Way!

In 1728, Margaret Dickson was already in her coffin when she came back to life after being . . .

a. hanged for murder.
b. run over by a stagecoach.
c. scalped.
d. thrown from her horse.

On the Fly: Angel Santana of New York City escaped unharmed when a robber's bullet bounced off his pant zipper.

Human Pipe Cleaner: In 1989, William Lamm of Vero Beach, California, escaped unhurt after he was sucked into a water intake pipe and traveled through it for 1,500 feet at 50 miles per hour.

Major Revival: In 1997, a Norwegian fisherman, Jan Egil Refsdahl, fell overboard in the North Atlantic Ocean. His heart stopped for four hours and his body temperature fell to 77ºF, yet he completely recovered.

Holy Smokestack! While repairing a high smokestack in Philadelphia, Pennsylvania, Dave Biddle fell ten stories, smashed through a concrete roof, and landed on a metal catwalk. His only injury was a broken ankle.

Had a Blast! A man from Kansas City, Missouri, decided to celebrate the Fourth of July with his friends. His neighbors were disturbed by the fireworks, so they called the police. Eager to hide the evidence, someone stashed the fireworks in the oven—and everyone forgot about them. Later, the man decided to bake some lasagna. When he turned the oven on, a huge explosion blew the kitchen to bits. Luckily, no one was hurt except for minor injuries caused by flying glass.

The Sky Is Falling!

Joanne and Mahlon Donovan of Derry, New Hampshire, were asleep in their home when a speeding car hit a hill, became airborne, and crashed into the Donovans' bedroom. The couple only survived because the car landed with one end propped up on a dresser, clearing their bed by a mere 12 inches.

No Way!

Old Man's Day is celebrated on October 2 in Hertfordshire, England, to commemorate the survival of Matthew Hall, a 16th-century farmer, who. . .

a. was trampled by a herd of stampeding dairy cows.
b. was revived when pallbearers accidentally dropped his coffin on the road.
c. rescued a family of ten from a burning farmhouse.
d. was struck by lightning on his 90th birthday.

Board to Death: In October 1991, John Ferreira of California survived a great white shark attack when he choked the shark by jamming his surfboard into its jaws.

A Lot at Stake: In the mid-1990s, Neil Pearson fell and impaled himself on a metal pipe used as a plant stake. The pipe went into his armpit, through his body, and out through his neck below his ear. X rays revealed that the stake missed his carotid artery and every vital organ in its path. Doctors say that if this freak accident were a medical procedure, it would have been deemed too risky. All Pearson needed was five stitches to close up the wound. He was released from the hospital the same day!

Jawbreaker: In 1963, Rodney Fox survived an attack by a 1,200-pound great white shark despite having sustained a wound in his side that required 462 stitches.

No Way!

When Wess Martin, foreman of a California ice plant, was accidentally locked in the company's icebox, he kept from freezing to death by . . .

a. doing 5,000 jumping jacks.
b. break dancing.
c. meditating.
d. pushing blocks of ice around.

Left a Bad Taste: In 1771, the *Boston Post* reported that an American harpooner named Jenkins was swallowed by a sperm whale when it snapped his whale boat in two with one bite. Jenkins disappeared into the huge jaws but must have disagreed with the whale—it spat him out right away. Jenkins was not hurt.

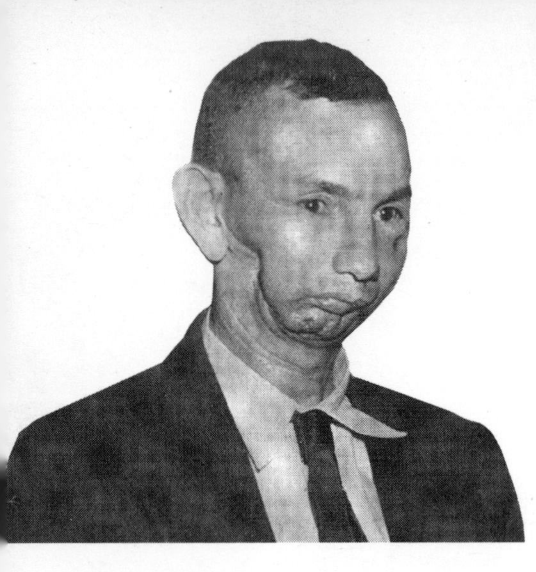

Bulletproof Man: On March 18, 1915, Wenseslao Moguel of Mérida, Mexico, survived execution by a firing squad—even after the final bullet was fired at close range to ensure a quick death.

All Fall Down! On July 17, 1990, Kelli Harrison and David Darrington of Australia had no sooner crossed London Bridge, a double arch in a seaside cliff caused by erosion, when they heard an enormous splash. When they looked back, they saw that the part of the land they'd just walked on had disappeared. The centuries-old arch had crumbled into the sea. Had the pair crossed 30 seconds later, they would have perished. Thankful to have survived their very close call, Harrison and Darrington were flown to safety by a police helicopter.

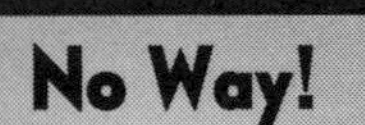

Moments after being shot in the chest by a would-be assassin, this United States president delivered a one-hour speech. His name was . . .

a. Theodore Roosevelt.
b. William Howard Taft.
c. Rutherford B. Hayes.
d. Thomas Jefferson.

The Human Cannonball: In 1782, an Indian holy man named Aruna, who angered the sultan of Mysore, was twice stuffed into a cannon and fired into the air. He survived both times. The first time, he was blown 800 feet and landed on the soft canopy atop an elephant. The second time, he fell without a scratch onto the thatched roof of a hut.

What a Crock! In the late 1960s, when a crocodile clamped down on the leg of a citizen of Tamative, Madagascar, the man grabbed hold of the crocodile's leg and won his freedom and his life after an hour-long tug-of-war.

Biting the Bull: When a pit bull clamped its vicelike jaws around the head of a young Scottish terrier on June 16, 2001, the terrier's owner, 73-year-old Margaret Hargrove of Tallahassee, Florida, sprang into action. She tried to pry open the pit bull's jaws but was unsuccessful. Not one to give up easily, Hargrove got down on her knees and bit the dog in the neck! The pit bull let go immediately, then bit Hargrove on the arm. Both owner and terrier needed stitches to close up their wounds.

No Way!

While attempting to parachute into Sumatra in 1997, Sergeant Cyril Jones crashed into the forest and was suspended in the trees for 12 days. He survived by eating . . .

a. all different kinds of bugs.
b. fruit brought to him by a monkey.
c. leaves he cut off with his pocketknife.
d. tree frogs and lizards.

You know what you have to do—find the fiction!

a. In 1997, Hurricane Pauline saved the lives of three people who had been lost at sea off the coast of Mexico for 15 days. The high winds swept them all safely back to shore!

Believe It! **Not!**

b. During the Middle Ages, French troops were spared an attack by the army of England's Edward III when 1,000 knights were killed by a rain of deadly hail.

Believe It! **Not!**

c. While taking part in a 1999 gliding exhibition at a local festival in Missouri, two pilots steered their planes into a gigantic thundercloud hoping the winds would boost them higher. No such luck! When the storm threatened to destroy their planes, the pilots jumped out into an updraft that kept them airborne long enough for a third plane to fly in and rescue them.

Believe It! **Not!**

d. During World War II, the United States Navy began studying ways of steering typhoons toward enemy ships. How did the Navy come up with the idea? Three of its own destroyers and nearly 800 men were lost in a typhoon in the Philippines on December 17, 1944.

Believe It! **Not!**

BONUS QUESTION

What role did the weather play in Christopher Columbus's voyage to the Americas?

a. Steady winds had been blowing the *Niña,* the *Pinta,* and the *Santa Maria* westward on their journey for so many days, the sailors were afraid the winds would never reverse and they'd never get home. But as the crews were plotting mutiny, the heavy waves from a powerful hurricane miles away convinced them there would be enough wind to get the ships back to Spain after their voyage of discovery was over. They abandoned their plans to take over the ships. Columbus survived and the fleet sailed onward to the Americas.

b. For years, there had been reports of sunken treasure only 100 miles off Columbus's course. Millions of dollars worth of gold and silver were believed to be aboard a Spanish armada that disappeared in a fierce cyclone in 1415. The crew wanted to look for the treasure when a new cyclone kicked up, almost capsizing the *Pinta* and taking the lives of several crew members. The surviving sailors decided to forget about the treasure and sail on.

c. The fleet was forced to ride out a dangerous hurricane for hours. When the winds finally died down, the crew realized the ships had been blown 500 miles closer to the land mass that would later be called the Americas.

It's not over yet. How many true rescues, survivor stories, and amazing escapes do you remember? Ready to find out? Circle your answers, and give yourself five points for each question you answer correctly.

1. In March 1989, Earth had a near miss with an asteroid the size of an aircraft carrier traveling at a speed of about 46,000 miles per hour. The extraterrestrial wrecking ball missed Earth by just six hours.

Believe It! **Not!**

2. Which of the following was *not* caused by the forces of nature?

a. A tornado changed the direction that water swirls in a toilet.

b. A volcano turned morning into night.

c. An earthquake forced part of the Mississippi River to flow upstream.

3. Which of the following was *not* caused by a bolt of lightning?

a. Sparks shot out of one man's fingers.

b. One man's body became magnetized, and large metal objects stuck to his limbs for the next six months.

c. One man's vision and hearing were suddenly restored after nine years of being blind and partially deaf.

4. The following are three tales of bizarre bird behavior. Which one is *not* true?

a. When a tornado trapped a red hen in a crate, she survived by eating her own eggs.

b. A mother duck alerted the police that her ducklings were trapped in a sewer by pulling on an officer's pant leg.

c. A heron rescued a goldfish that had jumped out of a pond.

5. Hold on—it's going to be one wild and crazy ride! Which one of the following amazing adventures is *not* true?

a. For six miles, two-year-old Allyson Hoary held onto the back of her dad's van, which was traveling at 60 miles per hour, until her dad saw her and pulled over.

b. Eight-year-old Deandra Anrig was carried 100 feet when her kite line got caught by a low-flying plane.

c. Five-year-old Freddie Lorenz sped downhill in a runaway grocery cart and across six lanes of street traffic until he finally crash-landed in some soft bushes.

6. An eight-year-old girl was carried 200 feet by a hawk before it dropped her into a nearby pond. She survived without injury!

Believe It! **Not!**

7. An airplane flew 275 miles and landed safely with 4,700 holes in its wings and fuselage. The holes were made by a flock of geese that had flown head-on into the plane.

Believe It! **Not!**

8. Frank Tower earned his place in the Ripley's files because he walked away from which unbelievable disasters?
a. Plane crashes in India, Japan, and China.
b. Three major shipwrecks, including the *Titanic.*
c. Three train wrecks, all within one year.

9. The lives of seven shipwrecked sailors were saved when their captain noticed that the seawater beneath their lifeboat changed color from blue to green as they drifted over a freshwater spring.

Believe It! **Not!**

10. Which of the following daring rescues never happened?
a. A surfer caught 17-month-old Sara Wolf when she fell overboard from a cruise ship.
b. A 12-year-old took the wheel of an out-of-control school bus, saving the lives of 33 kids on board.
c. A bus driver saved 30 passengers when he jammed his legs under the wheels to keep the bus from rolling over a cliff.

11. In 1991, a pod of dolphins performed which amazing rescue?
a. They saved eight passengers from a capsized yacht in California by carrying them to shore on their backs.
b. They protected a group of shipwrecked sailors from circling sharks in Florida.
c. They used their bodies to plug a large hole at the waterline of a sinking boat in New York's North River, saving hundreds of passengers.

12. Only one of the following daring doggy rescues is true. Can you pick out which one?

a. A Newfoundland dog swam to shore with a lifeline gripped in his teeth, ultimately saving 92 people from a wrecked ship that was breaking up in the stormy seas.

b. A golden retriever lay down in the middle of the road until a truck stopped. She then led the driver to her home where her owner was passed out on the floor.

c. A Chihuahua attacked a crocodile that had chomped down on the arm of her four-year-old owner.

13. Snail slime on the tracks can cause a train to derail.

Believe It! **Not!**

14. Which of the following embarrassing situations is *not* true?

a. A man had to be rescued by firefighters when his tongue stuck to the inside of a freezer.

b. A man had to be rushed to the hospital after getting a curling iron stuck to his scalp.

c. A little girl had to be rescued by paramedics after she kissed her pet turtle and it wouldn't let go of her lip.

15. Which of the following shark stories is really true?

a. A surfer survived an attack by a great white shark by jamming his surfboard between the shark's jaws.

b. When a shark bit down on a swimmer's leg in northern Rhodesia, the swimmer clamped his teeth down on the tip of the shark's nose until it let go.

c. A scuba diver near Acapulco, Mexico, survived an attack by a ten-foot shark by swimming directly into the shark's mouth, past its jaws, and into its gullet.

Answer Key

Chapter 1

No Way!

Page 5: **d.** moaning camel.
Page 7: **a.** chasing it on horseback and lashing at it with a whip.
Page 8: **c.** sporting a bad haircut.
Page 11: **d.** supply all of Arizona with electricity.
Page 13 **b.** red spider spinning its web.
Page 15: **b.** cover all of Manhattan to a depth of 28 stories.
Page 16: **c.** horses refused to eat.
Page 19: **d.** one million.
Page 20: **b**. Galveston, Texas.

Brain Buster: **c.** is false.
Bonus Question: **b.**

Chapter 2

No Way!

Page 23: **b.** carried it down a ladder.
Page 25: **c.** from a seven-story apartment building.
Page 27: **a.** lunged for a football and landed on a pencil that pierced his heart.
Page 29: **c.** a freight train passed over her body.
Page 31: **b.** using his drum as a life raft.
Page 32: **c.** accidentally going over Niagara Falls.

Brain Buster: **d.** is false.
Bonus Question: **b.**

Chapter 3

No Way!

Page 35: **a.** boat.

Page 36: **d.** he mistook the *Titanic*'s emergency flares for fireworks.

Page 39: **c.** a salmon (that was dropped by an eagle crashing through the windshield.

Page 41: **b.** windmill.

Page 43: **b.** everyone had been rescued.

Page 44: **c.** whistling.

Brain Buster: **a.** is false.

Bonus Question: **a.**

Chapter 4

No Way!

Page 47: **c.** canary.

Page 49: **c.** the dams built by 60 beaver colonies.

Page 51: **b.** an albatross.

Page 53: **b.** kites.

Page 55: **a.** the short circuit set off the doorbell, jarring him awake.

Page 56: **c.** tying off a bleeding artery with dental floss.

Brain Buster: **b.** is false.

Bonus Question: **c.**

Chapter 5

No Way!

Page 59: **b.** coughed up the bullet.
Page 61: **a.** brain.
Page 63: **a.** her petticoat opened like a parachute.
Page 65: **a.** hanged for murder.
Page 67: **b.** was revived when pallbearers accidentally dropped his coffin on the road.
Page 69: **d.** pushing blocks of ice around.
Page 70: **a.** Theodore Roosevelt.
Page 72: **b.** fruit brought to him by a monkey.

Brain Buster: **c.** is false.

Bonus Question: **a.**

Pop Quiz

1. **Believe It!**
2. **a.**
3. **b.**
4. **c.**
5. **c.**
6. **Not!**
7. **Not!**
8. **b.**
9. **Believe It!**
10. **a.**
11. **b.**
12. **a.**
13. **Believe It!**
14. **b.**
15. **a.**

What's Your Ripley's Rank?

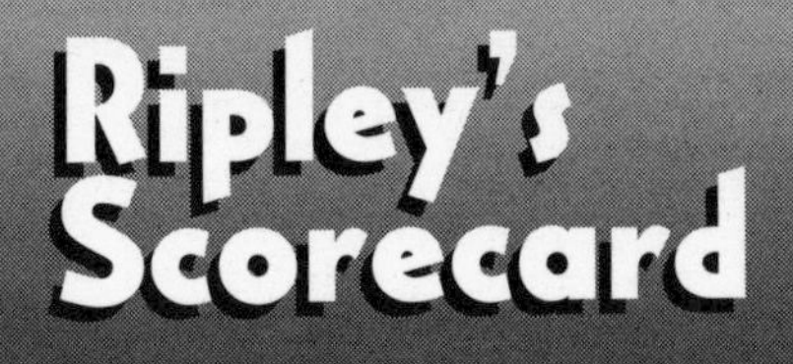

Ripley's Scorecard

Congrats! You've busted your brain over some of the oddest human behavior in the world and proven your ability to tell fact from fiction. Now it's time to rate your Ripley's knowledge. Are you an amazing survivor or an extreme escapist? Check out the answers in the answer key, and use this page to keep track of how many trivia questions you've answered correctly. Then add 'em up and find out how you rate.

Here's the scoring breakdown—give yourself:

★ **10 points** for every **No Way!** you answered correctly;

★ **20 points** for every fiction you spotted in the **Ripley's Brain Busters**;

★ **10** for every **Bonus Question** you answered right;

★ and **5** for every **Pop Quiz** question you answered correctly.

Here's a tally sheet:

Number of **No Way!** questions answered correctly:	_____ x 5	= _____
Number of **Ripley's Brain Buster** questions answered correctly:	_____ x 10	= _____
Number of **Bonus Questions** answered correctly:	_____ x 5	= _____
Chapter Total:		_____

Write your totals for each chapter and the Pop Quiz section in the spaces below. Then add them up to get your FINAL SCORE. Your FINAL SCORE decides how you rate:

Chapter 1 Total: ________
Chapter 2 Total: ________
Chapter 3 Total ________
Chapter 4 Total: ________
Chapter 5 Total: ________
Pop Quiz Total: ________

FINAL SCORE: ________

525–301

Amazing Survivor!

You don't need to check with friends or look online to know you're right. You can tell the difference between fact and fiction on your own—no matter how bizarre the choices. You make it past the Bonus Round every time and you come out on top. You are the big winner, a breakout star, and a true survivor. You know a thing or two about surviving some tough challenges and you can't be fooled. If they passed out trophies for fiction detection, you'd win the lifetime achievement award. You ARE amazing. *Believe It!*

300–201

Escape Artist

You don't fall for tricks or teasers. You know what's up—the truth is the truth and you have an amazing ability to spot it. Exaggerations can't fool you, gossip doesn't throw you, and rumors are just rumors in your world. You love a good escape-from-danger story—they're inspiring and you know it. But you also know when you are being duped. You escape the trip ups with style. And you're rising in the ranks. Keep it up!

200–101

Close Call

You've escaped the ranks of the truly out of touch—but just barely. Don't give up. Your internal fact-checker may need some fine-tuning, but that's not a problem! The world is full of amazingly true tales as well as tantalizing tall tales. So you'll always have opportunities to test your Ripley's radar. Now you've got experience. New challenges lie ahead. Can you deal?

100–0

Extreme Escapist

You are in serious need of a Ripley's rescue! You have a hard time figuring out if someone is speaking in earnest or just pulling your leg. People like to tease you by getting you to believe outrageous tales of escape and rescue. That's okay. Maybe it's just not your thing, maybe you're too trusting, or maybe you just don't care. Whatever the reason, just keep in mind that the truth really can be stranger than fiction—and the world is constantly proving it!

Photo Credits

Ripley Entertainment Inc. and the editors of this book wish to thank the following photographers, agents, and other individuals for permission to use and reprint the following photographs in this book. Any photographs included in this book that are not acknowledged below are property of the Ripley Archives. Great effort has been made to obtain permission from the owners of all materials included in this book. Any errors that may have been made are unintentional and will gladly be corrected in future printings if notice is sent to Ripley Entertainment Inc., 5728 Major Boulevard, Orlando, Florida 32819.

Black & White Photos

7 Malagash Cottage/Tom McCoag/Reprinted with permission from The Halifax Herald Limited

8 Johnstown Flood/National Park Service

9 Asteroid/NASA Photo Gallery

10 Peekskill Meteorite/Allan Lang/R. A. Langheinrich Meteorites/Ilion, New York/www.nyrockman.com;

10 Lightning; 37 Skydiver; 53 Dolphins/CORBIS

12 Mount Pelée/Copyright Unknown

14 Mauna Loa/U.S.G.S. Photo Library, Denver, Colorado

15 Mount Saint Helens/Austin Post, U.S.G.S./CVO/Glaciology Project

17 Anchorage Earthquake/NOAA: National Geophysical Data Center, Boulder, Colorado

18 Mississippi River; 27 Black Cat; 38 Amsterdam Canal; 64 Tower of London/PhotoDisc

40 *Andrea Doria*/Associated Press

42 *Endurance*/Frank Hurley/1914–16 Imperial Trans-Antarctic Expedition/ Royal Geographical Society Picture Library

50 Jambo/James Morgan/© Durrell Wildlife Conservation Trust

55 Fawn; 59 Coral Snake/Copyright 2001, Ripley Entertainment and its licensors

61 Sperm Whale/© 2000 Jonathan Bird/Oceanic Research Group, Inc.

63 George Washington Carver/Iowa State University/Special Collections Department

Color Insert

Anchorage Earthquake/NOAA: National Geophysical Data Center, Boulder, Colorado

Chicago Fire/Chicago Historical Society/View of people racing over the Randolph Bridge for their lives/Lithograph ICHi-02961; Lithographer Kellogg & Bulkeley, 1871

Dolphins; Parrot/Copyright 2001 Ripley Entertainment and its licensors

Hamster; Goldfish/PhotoDisc

Jambo/James Morgan/© Durrell Wildlife Conservation Trust

Joachim Degaway and Daughter/Palani Mohan/*The Age*

Lulu; Jim Symancky; Stuart Diver; *Andrea Doria* and Survivor; Air India Crash/Associated Press

Mount Pelée/Copyright unknown

Paricutín; Mauna Loa; Mt. Mayon/U.S.G.S. Photo Library, Denver, Colorado

Valzur Avalanche; Sarno Mudslides; Selby Trainwreck/Reuters Picture Agency

Cover

Shark/© James D. Watt Photography

Paricutín/U.S.G.S. Photo Library, Denver, Colorado

Odd-inary People

In this astounding album of the most incredible individuals on Earth, you'll meet a teenager who can pull a pickup truck filled with her high school football team, a Manchurian farmer who had a 13-inch horn growing from the back of his head, and a woman who had 240 operations to sculpt her face into the likeness of an ancient Egyptian queen. These are just a few of the unusual men, women, and children that fill the pages of **Odd-inary People**—people whose uniqueness is bound to amaze you!

Coming soon . . .

Incredible Inventions

Get the inside scoop on the world's most bizarre inventions, like the flying automobile, the grass-covered suit, Thomas Edison's cement furniture, "Roller Man's" body-suit on wheels, and more!